Ɵ 8

TRAPPED
IN THE
SIXTIES

SUSANNAH BRIN

TAKE TEN BOOKS

BY SUSANNAH BRIN

Development and Production: Laurel Associates, Inc.
Cover Illustrator: Black Eagle Productions

© 1998 Saddleback Publishing, Inc.

SADDLEBACK
PUBLISHING • INC.

3505 Cadillac Ave., Building F-9
Costa Mesa, CA 92626

ISBN 1-56254-235-4

Printed in the United States of America
03 02 01 MM 01 00 CM 99 98   8 7 6 5 4 3 2 1

Contents

Chapter 1

Johnny Brown slouched down the stairs to the kitchen. He could hear his sister's voice rising and falling with excitement. Shaking his head, he frowned. Johnny wondered how she could be excited about *anything* in this awful, hick place!

Johnny hated Laird's Junction. It wasn't even a town—just a dot on the map, really. All of Main Street was one short block long. There was just a cafe and a little general store with two gas pumps out in front. There wasn't even a school, for Pete's sake. The only schools were twenty minutes away in the slightly bigger town of Meridian.

Laird's Junction was just the kind of place his parents had dreamed of when they had lived in L.A. So here they had come. Now, stuck in the middle of nowheresville, Johnny grumbled as he made his way past a stack of unpacked boxes on his way to the kitchen.

"Morning, honey. Sleep well?" asked his mother. The pretty woman turned from the pancakes she was flipping and gave him a big smile.

"Not very. I can't get used to how quiet it is out here," he grumbled. Pulling out a chair, he sat down opposite his sister, giving her a frown.

"Right, like you really miss the sounds of distant gunfire in the night," mocked his sister. She rolled her blue eyes and he shot her another frown.

Claire was a shorter, blonder version of himself—or so everyone said. He didn't see the resemblance, except maybe in the eyes. They both had their mother's big blue eyes. But that was it as far as he was concerned.

"Well, I for one don't miss Los

Angeles," said Johnny's father. "I don't miss the smog, and I certainly don't miss that awful commute! It used to take me an hour to get to the hospital. Now I have only a twenty-minute drive over to Meridian General. In another five minutes, I'm ready to see patients," said Johnny's father. Grinning, the tall, lanky man stood up and reached for his jacket.

"I'm glad for you, Dad. I just wish you could have waited until after I graduated to make this move. It was only one more year," said Johnny.

Dr. Brown heard the edge of anger in his son's voice. "When the position at this hospital came available, I had to jump on it. You know that. We talked it over and we all decided together— remember?" said his father, giving the boy his full attention.

"Yeah," said Johnny, glancing away from the worried look in his father's eyes. The last thing he wanted to do was cause trouble. His father had already had one heart attack—partly from the strain of working in a big city hospital. The overload of patients had been too much stress for him. "But it's just that it is so *boring* here."

"I've got an idea, son. Why don't you fire up the new tractor? You could cut the grass on the back pasture," suggested Johnny's father.

Johnny nodded, but was thinking dark thoughts. Mowing the back pasture would be about as much fun as having the flu. But he would do it.

After Johnny's father left, his mother placed a stack of pancakes in front of him. Then she sat down herself, with a cup of coffee. "Don't look so glum, Johnny. You'll make friends here when school starts in the fall. Maybe even this summer. Claire has already met a couple of girls down at Roamer's Rest."

"What's Roamer's Rest?" Johnny asked. He wasn't really interested, but he was glad to get the conversation off himself. Sighing, he forked a hunk of pancake into his mouth.

"You'd like it, dear. It's a park with a river running through it. There's a pretty spot where the river widens out. Everyone goes swimming there."

"And there's a dock that everyone dives from," Claire chimed in. Her blue eyes danced with mischief as she added, "At night the park turns into a lover's lane."

"Claire! Where did you hear such a thing?" their mother cried, trying not to show her amusement.

"My new friend Sally told me. She says everyone sits in their cars and makes out. If you ever get a girlfriend you could take her over there, Johnny," Claire teased.

"Why don't you just drop dead?" Johnny snorted in disgust. Why couldn't his sister keep her nose out of his business? He pushed his plate away. Crossing the kitchen, he slammed out the back door.

Johnny began wondering what the girls would be like at his new school. He hoped there were some pretty ones. But he figured he wouldn't have much of a chance, being the new guy in town. He'd had a girlfriend back in Los Angeles, but she'd called it off. She didn't want a long-distance relationship. He had felt bad about it, but what could he do? Nothing.

Walking past the shiny new tractor, Johnny pulled open the heavy barn doors. The hot July sun streamed into the dark interior. Overhead, he could hear the rustling and fluttering of wings. He guessed it was the doves and barn owls resettling on the rafters. The pale light lay like ribbons across the bales of hay. Johnny smelled dust and the musty odor of rotting straw. *I bet no one's been in here since the Baers moved out thirty years ago*, he thought to himself.

Broken tools and rusted parts of all kinds of farming equipment lay in piles everywhere. Old bales of hay sagged on top of each other in ceiling-high stacks. Then Johnny saw a canvas tarp covering a very large object at the very back of the barn.

What do we have here? Another tractor? he wondered. He pulled at a corner of the tarp. Bits of straw and dust and grit flew into the air. Finally the old tarp fell away, revealing a dusty old black car!

"Wow! It's a *muscle* car!" Johnny exclaimed. He slowly ran his fingers across the metal nameplate on the rear fender of the car. It read *GTO*. Johnny had seen a few on the freeway. And his father had often talked about how the Pontiac GTO was one of the fastest cars on the road back in the late 1960s.

Johnny walked around the car several times, inspecting it from every angle. The car had bucket seats and a four-on-the-floor transmission. Oh, sure, it was pretty beat up. The back window was busted out, and the front fender on the passenger's side was dented. The interior was dirtier than a pigpen. But all in all, it looked like it was in pretty good shape.

Sliding behind the wheel, Johnny imagined himself driving into the parking lot at his new school. In his daydream, the GTO's engine was purring like a cat. Everyone turned to look at him as the car's dual exhausts rumbled menacingly, announcing his arrival.

Chapter 2

By late in the afternoon, Johnny had finished mowing the pasture behind the barn. Parking the big tractor near the back door, he jumped down and ran toward the kitchen. Hot and tired, he wiped the back of his hand across his forehead, streaking his face with sweat and dirt.

As he went into the house, he let the screen door bang behind him. "Hey, Mom! Claire? Is anyone here?" No answer. *They must have gone into Laird's Junction or over to Roamer's Rest*, he told himself. Now that he thought about it, he wouldn't mind going for a swim himself. It was hotter than a furnace outside the house.

He grabbed a bottle of lemonade from the refrigerator and then stood by the sink, drinking it. His mouth was dry, and the cold liquid felt good. As he finished off the lemonade, he stared out the window at the barn. He thought about the black car sitting in there.

An idea had come to him while he was out working on the tractor. *It wouldn't take much to fix up the car.* His dad had been promising to buy him a car. Well, now he wouldn't have to. There was already a car out in the barn. It seemed like it was just waiting for him.

He put the empty lemonade bottle on the countertop and headed back outside. Climbing up onto the tractor, he shifted into reverse and started backing toward the barn. The sound of the tractor's engine roared in his ears as he inched the machine up to the back bumper of the GTO. Leaving the tractor running, he jumped down and searched the barn for something to use as a tow line. *That should do the trick,* he thought, spying a length of chain lying in a heap near a huge roll of rusted barbed wire.

He hooked the chain to the rear axle of the Pontiac. Then he secured it to the tractor's trailer hitch. After putting the car in neutral and making sure the parking brake was off, Johnny climbed back on the tractor. The floor groaned as the tractor lurched forward. Slowly, it started pulling the car behind. After a few minutes, Johnny had towed the car to the driveway behind the house.

Johnny walked around the car, studying it from different angles. *It needs a new back window and some new tires,* he said to himself, taking inventory. *And I'll need to pound out the grill on the passenger's side where it's dented—and get a new headlight, too.*

That shouldn't be too hard. He walked around to the driver's side and opened the door.

Sliding behind the wheel, Johnny flipped down the visor to see if a key was hidden there. Nothing. It wasn't there, and there was nothing in the glovebox, either. The he noticed a bump in the smooth surface of the floor mat. He lifted the mat and grinned. *Bingo*, he said to himself as he picked up a set of keys.

Johnny slipped the key into the ignition and gave it a twist. He didn't really expect anything to happen. The car must have been sitting there for years! But suddenly the powerful engine roared to life. Johnny couldn't believe it. The battery should have died *years* ago! "This is incredible," he said aloud.

As Johnny gripped the steering wheel, he could feel the mighty hum of the engine. It was like a powerful beast trying to break free of its restraints. He gunned the engine several times and laughed at the rumble of the mufflerless motor. To Johnny's ears, the big car actually seemed to growl!

Leaving the motor idling, Johnny got out to inspect the GTO's engine. He popped the hood and stared down at the motor. Again, he was surprised. In fact, he was absolutely speechless. The engine was as shiny and clean as the day it had rolled off the assembly line. *How could this be?* There was no logical explanation for it.

As Johnny studied the engine, his mother and sister drove into the yard. Claire, her hair still wet from swimming, walked all around the car. She ran her finger across the hood, making a streak in the car's dusty surface. "This old clunker must be a hundred years old."

"What do you know? It isn't that old. It was built in the sixties," Johnny snorted. He gave her a pitying look. "You are so lame," he said.

"Well, where in the world did this car come from?" asked his mother, coming to stand by his side.

"I found it in the barn. It was way in the back—under an old tarp. Isn't it *great*, mom?" said Johnny, speaking a mile a minute in his excitement. "Do you think Dad will let me keep it?"

"I don't know why not. But why would you want a car as old as this one?" his mother asked.

"Yeah, I thought you wanted a Honda," Claire said. Then she edged past the open driver's-side door and slid into the seat. She glanced around, then adjusted the rearview mirror so she could see herself.

"Hey, what do you think you're doing?" snapped Johnny. Crossing quickly to the driver's side, he reached past his sister to switch off the ignition. "Come on, Claire, get out."

"No fighting, you two," said their mother. "Claire, why don't you come in the house now? You should hang up your wet suit and towel. Leave your brother alone now."

Claire made a face at Johnny as she got out of the car. "I didn't want to sit in this icky old car anyway," she said in a huff. Then she flounced off toward the house with their mother.

"Good," Johnny grumbled. He was surprised at how possessive he was beginning to feel about the car. It was weird—like he was falling in love with it. Closing the hood, he squatted down to inspect the fender and broken headlight on the passenger's side. *I can pound this out*, he thought to himself. He ran his hand lovingly along the broken curve of the headlight socket.

"Soon you'll be as good as new," he whispered. Then he rose and walked slowly around the car.

When Johnny looked up, he saw Claire heading his way again. *Oh, no,* he thought. *Why can't that little pest just get lost and leave me alone?*

"I was thinking that maybe I could help you wash your car," said Claire. Smiling, she held up a bucket of soapy water and a bunch of rags. Johnny saw that it was a peace offering.

"I thought you didn't like this car. You called it a clunker," said Johnny.

"Well, I didn't mean it," said Claire. She cocked her head to one side and smiled again. "Anyway, it will look a hundred times better once it's washed."

Seeing the hopeful expression on her face almost made Johnny laugh. She was trying to be nice—as nice as a thirteen-year-old kid sister could be, anyway. "All right, I'll get the hose. But you'll have to be careful, Claire. Don't get any water near that busted-out window. I don't want the interior getting wet."

"I'll be careful," promised Claire. She reached into the bucket and pulled out a soapy sponge. In less than a minute she was happily washing the hood of the car.

Together, they worked their way around the car. Claire soaped and scrubbed, and Johnny hosed off the soap. When she reached the rear quarter panel on the driver's side, Claire found a crusted patch of dried dirt. The sponge wouldn't wash it off. Using her fingers like a scraper, Claire finally loosened the dry dirt. She was surprised to see that red letters had appeared underneath. Leaning closer for a better look, she rubbed the sponge even harder on the spot. "Johnny, look at this! Your car has a *name*!"

Johnny dropped the hose and stepped closer. Claire was right. Written in a flowery script of blood-red paint was the name "Johnny B."

"Imagine that, Johnny! Whoever owned this car had the same first name as you do. And the same last initial," breathed Claire. She seemed a little awed by the fact. "It's sort of spooky, isn't it?"

"Why do you say that? The people who used to own this place were named Baer," Johnny said quickly. It was a coincidence and nothing more, he told himself. No big deal. After all, Johnny was a common name.

Chapter 3

By the first week in August, Johnny had the GTO in perfect running condition. The rear window had been replaced. The front fender and headlight had been repaired. And he had bought four new tires.

The only thing I have left to do is give the car a good waxing, Johnny thought. Quickly, he gulped down a glass of orange juice and got up from the breakfast table.

"So, son, are you going to take your car for a test drive today?" asked his father. The tall man was standing at the open back door, getting ready to leave for the hospital.

"Yeah," answered Johnny, crossing to where his father stood looking out.

"Can I go?" Claire piped up.

Ignoring her, Johnny turned to his father. "I thought I would give the car a good waxing this morning. It's a great old car. It deserves to look its best when it goes out on the street."

Johnny's father smiled and gave Mrs. Brown a wink. "I think you're falling in love with that car, son."

Johnny ducked his head, feeling a hot blush of embarrassment rush to his face.

His father slapped him on the back and grinned. "Nothing wrong with caring about a car. I remember when I got my first car. It was a '54 Chevy—sky blue and white. That was one of the best days of my life."

"I remember, too," said Johnny's mother. "Your father washed and waxed that car so much I thought he was going to scrub the paint off!" She walked from the table to the sink and looked out the window. "Well, you'd better get at your waxing before the sun gets too hot. They say it's going to hit a hundred and four today."

"Can I go swimming at Roamer's Rest this afternoon, Mom?" begged Claire. The girl flashed her mother a pleading look.

"I'm sorry, honey. I promised to help out at the hospital today."

"Maybe Johnny could take me when he finishes waxing his car," said Claire. She gave her brother her sweetest smile.

"I don't know if I'll have time," answered Johnny as he followed his father out the door. The last thing he wanted to do was drive Claire around. But he knew better than to say so in front of his parents.

The heat of the morning rose steadily as Johnny waxed his way around the car. By the time he reached the rear of the car, his T-shirt was soaked with sweat. He pulled it off and waited for the air to cool his skin. He was glad he had parked the GTO in the shade of the large apple tree. At least he had *some* relief from the sun. But the heat was so intense that it dried the wax as fast as he put it on. Johnny's muscles ached from working so hard to rub off the crusty wax. He shook his arms to lessen the pain.

Only this rear section to do, and then I'm done, he told himself. He started to dab the wax around the rear window frame.

As he rubbed in the wax, he felt a row of small pockmarks on the metal that he hadn't noticed before. Now he leaned in for a closer look. Scattered around the frame were dozens of small, round indentations. *That's weird*, he thought. *I wonder what made these strange little pockmarks?*

"What are you looking at?" asked Claire, walking over to watch him.

Johnny glanced at her and sighed.

She was wearing her swimsuit and a pair of cutoffs. Their mother had left hours ago. It could only mean that Claire was expecting him to take her to Roamer's Rest. Knowing that she wasn't going to go away, he pointed at a patch of pockmarks. "Look at these funny-looking dents, Claire. I don't know how they could have gotten here."

Claire studied the spots. "Probably they were always there and you didn't notice them. You can't really see them unless you look real close."

"Yeah," Johnny agreed. But still the dents bothered him. The harder he worked, the more he wanted the car to be *perfect*.

"Wow, your car's so shiny I can see myself," said Claire. She bent down and looked at her reflection shining from the door panel.

"It does look good, doesn't it?" Johnny grinned and stood back, admiring the GTO. The sleek black body shone like polished marble. Dad said that the car was a 1965 model. But Johnny thought it looked as modern and as fresh as any car on the road.

"Are you almost done?" asked Claire, sweetly.

"I just have to finish the trunk," answered Johnny. He started rubbing off the wax that had already started to dry.

"Sure is hot today," said Claire, glancing up at the sun. She fanned her face with her hand. "Sure would feel good to go swimming."

"Yeah," agreed Johnny, giving the trunk of the car one last swipe with his rag. He stepped back to admire his work. He knew that Claire was angling for a ride. "It's a long walk down to Roamer's Rest in this heat."

Claire's eyes flashed. She couldn't tell if he was teasing her or not. "I could do it," she said defiantly.

Johnny bit his lip to keep from grinning. "Really? Then why are you hanging around here? Get walking."

Claire stomped her foot and turned to go. "Fine! I'll walk." But she hadn't gone more than a few feet when she turned back. "Please, Johnny, won't you give me a ride in your car? *You* could go swimming, too. You know how hot and miserable it is. Please?"

Johnny couldn't help laughing. Claire sure had a way of getting what she wanted. But he also admitted to himself that the thought of going swimming sounded pretty good to him, too. "Okay. Get in."

Johnny turned the key in the ignition, and the big V8 engine roared to life. Johnny grinned. He loved the thundering sound of the motor. He shifted into first, accelerated, and the car leapt forward.

Claire buckled her seatbelt and

squirmed around, trying hard to get comfortable in the leather bucket seat. "These seatbelts are sure old fashioned, but I like them better than the shoulder harnesses we have today."

Johnny searched for oncoming cars before he turned out of the farmhouse drive onto the one-lane highway. Once they were on the road, he rolled down his window, rested his elbow on the window frame, and settled back to enjoy the drive. Warm air ruffled his hair and blew lightly against his face. He felt like he was on top of the world.

"Can I turn on the radio?" asked Claire.

"Go ahead and try it. I don't know if it works."

"I can't believe you haven't tried the radio! It's the most important part of a car," said Claire, shaking her head as she switched it on. Static scratched at their ears like fingernails on a chalkboard. Quickly, she turned the volume down and then began punching buttons, looking for a station. The radio dial jumped from number to number. More static.

"It works. Too bad there aren't any stations around here," sighed Johnny. "Face it, Sis—we live in nowheresville."

"That's not true. On Mom's car radio the other day, I got five stations to come in. One station was from San Francisco. It played the top ten, hiphop, and rap."

"Oh, I'll bet Mom just loves rap," laughed Johnny.

Claire made a face as she continued punching buttons, looking for a station. Then suddenly the static disappeared. Now Roger Miller was singing "King of the Road."

"Boy, *that's* an old song. Must be from the sixties," said Johnny, shifting into fourth as he approached a long stretch of flat, open road. The GTO shot forward like an unleashed animal.

"That's you, Johnny—King of the Road," giggled Claire, pushing another button on the radio. "It's been a hard day's night, and I've been . . ." sang the Beatles. Again, Claire switched the dial. Another sixties song came on. This time it was Ray Peterson crooning, "Tell Laura I love her."

"This is really *strange.* First I can't get any stations to come in, and now the only ones I get are playing sixties music," said Claire, frowning as she kept punching buttons.

"Here, let me do it," said Johnny impatiently. He punched one of the silver buttons and the Crystals' "He's a Rebel" blared out. He hit another button and Lesley Gore was singing "It's My Party." What was going on? In frustration, Johnny switched off the radio.

"I know what's happening. Your car is a sixties car, so the radio can only play sixties music. It's like those old *Twilight Zone* shows or a Stephen King book," teased Claire, her blue eyes dancing with merriment.

"Yeah, right," snapped Johnny. "Or maybe all the stations are into playing 'oldies but goodies.' You ever think of that?" He downshifted and turned toward Roamer's Rest. *Claire's an idiot*, he told himself. Still, it was downright *weird* that all the stations were playing only songs from the sixties.

Chapter 4

Johnny followed Claire through the shady park. Down at the river, kids were splashing in the cool water and running along the old wooden dock. Here and there at picnic tables, mothers talked as they kept an eye on their children. Claire introduced Johnny to her friend Sally, a freckle-faced skinny girl who giggled shyly. Soon the two girls walked off to sun themselves on the riverbank.

Johnny looked around. He didn't see anyone his own age, but he didn't care. He dove off the dock and swam across to the other side of the pool. Beyond the roped-off swimming hole, he could see that the river narrowed and rippled over a rocky surface.

Johnny liked the feel of the sun on his back. For a while, he floated in the water and stared up at the cloudless blue sky. He wished one of his friends from Los Angeles was there. He really missed his friends.

He wondered what they would think of his car. One of these days, maybe he would drive it down to L.A. Most of his old friends were into Hondas. He had wanted one, too—until he had found the GTO. Now nothing could compare to the muscle car.

He crawled back up on the wooden dock and glanced over at the parking lot. There his car sat in the shade, like a panther waiting to pounce. Johnny smiled. It was too cool for words. He lay down on his stomach and soon fell asleep, the lapping of the water and the shrieking of kids in his ears.

"Wake up, sleepyhead," said Claire, pushing at his side with her bare foot.

"Go away," mumbled Johnny,

without opening his eyes.

"Okay, but you'll be sorry. You're getting red as a lobster," chirped Claire.

"Oh, all right, all right," Johnny groaned, looking up at his sister. He saw that she had her cutoffs back on and her towel folded under her arm. "I suppose you're ready to go now?"

"Yes. Sally's already left, and I'm getting sort of bored. You've been asleep for two hours."

Johnny was surprised he'd slept so long. He yawned and stood up. Claire was right about his back getting a sunburn. He could already feel a stinging heat across his shoulders. "Let's go, then," he said as he started toward the parking lot.

The interior of the GTO was hot when they got in. Johnny quickly shifted into reverse and gave it some gas, making the car lurch backward, spraying loose gravel as it went. Peeling out of the lot, Johnny fishtailed the car as it moved from gravel to blacktop.

"Stop it! You're driving like a *maniac!*" scolded Claire.

"I am not," grinned Johnny. He was pleased with how well he could handle the car. He liked its quick steering and stiff suspension.

"Yes you are, Johnny. You're acting just like some showoff hot-rodder."

Johnny rolled his eyes. "That was nothing. I wasn't even going ten miles an hour."

"Well, just don't go fast," instructed Claire. Her mouth was set in a straight line of disapproval.

Glancing at her out of the corner of his eye, he thought she looked exactly like their mother when she got upset. He knew Claire wouldn't like what he was going to do next—but he didn't care. He pressed his foot down on the gas pedal, and the GTO shot forward in a burst of speed.

"Johnny!" screamed Claire, "I'm warning you. I'll get sick."

He grinned at his sister as the speedometer needle inched up to sixty-five, seventy, seventy-five. Then, worrying that she might get sick and mess up his nice clean car, he slowed to forty. "Is this speed okay with you?" he asked, unable to keep the teasing edge from his voice.

"Yes," answered Claire, shooting him another dark look.

"What a chicken you are, Claire," Johnny said. "Don't you want to see how fast this baby can go?" The truth was that he wanted to know himself. He wanted to push the gas pedal all the way to the floor, to feel the car burn up the miles.

"No, thank you! Mom says you have to be careful on these country roads. She says you never know when a tractor or a bunch of cows will be crossing the road," Claire went on.

Then she reached for the radio and switched it on. Roger Miller's song, "King of the Road," was playing again.

"Hey, there's my song," laughed Johnny. He put his hand over the radio's buttons so she couldn't change the station.

"Right," answered Claire, slouching down in her seat. "We're trapped in the sixties."

Johnny glanced over and saw that Claire looked sad. "Hey, what's wrong with you?"

"Nothing." She stared out of the window.

"Come on. Something's wrong."

"I miss my friends. Sally is nice, but it's not like being with my *old* girl-friends. You know what I mean?"

"Yeah, I know," answered Johnny, wondering what his buddies in L.A. were doing right now. "Look, why don't we go into Laird's Junction and get a root beer float or something?"

"Okay," said Claire, sitting up a little straighter. "I could go for some french fries and a coke."

As they turned off toward Laird's Junction, heat waves rose from the one-lane highway that snaked its way through endless, stubbled fields. On the radio, the Dixie Cups sang "Chapel Of Love." Claire giggled and mimicked the singers. Johnny smiled and turned up the volume.

Up ahead was an old cemetery. Just beyond that and around a sharp curve in the road was a huge old oak tree. Johnny noticed that halfway up the trunk, someone had carved a giant X into the bark. "Hey, Claire, look at that X," he yelled over the music.

Claire nodded and yelled back. "X marks the spot, I guess. Maybe there's money buried at the root of the tree—like in those old pirate movies."

"You watch too much TV," Johnny answered with a grin. "It's probably just a warning. Looks like a good place for an accident."

Johnny began turning into the curve. Then without warning Claire's door popped open. She screamed in surprise but then grabbed the handle and pulled the door shut.

Johnny slammed on the brakes and grabbed his sister's arm. "Are you all right?"

"Yeah," Claire replied shakily. "But that was *too* weird."

Johnny was about to reply, but as he started the car moving again, the engine suddenly revved and the gas pedal seemed to press itself to the floor! Johnny took his foot from the gas and braked, but nothing happened. The speedometer needle kept rising. It shot past eighty, then ninety, and then a hundred. By now the gas pedal had pressed itself flat against the floor!

"Johnny, what are you doing? *Stop*!" Claire screamed. Her eyes were wide with fear and she gripped the edges of her seat. "I'm trying to!" Johnny yelled.

Johnny tried to downshift, but the stick wouldn't budge from fourth gear. The car rocketed down the road at 110 miles an hour. Then, about a quarter of a mile down the highway, the GTO came to a screeching halt. Johnny switched off the radio and took a deep breath. He could feel the adrenalin pumping through his body.

"I can't *believe* you, Johnny," Claire cried. "Do you want to get us both killed?" Johnny saw that her face was pinched and white with fear. "The gas pedal was stuck," he said, trying to convince himself that was really what had happened.

What could he say? There was no other explanation. Gripping the steering wheel, he could feel the car's engine idling like a throbbing heart.

Chapter 5

Johnny drove the short distance into Laird's Junction without further trouble. He parked in front of an old cafe, a low-slung wooden building in need of paint. On the two large plate-glass windows facing the street it said, *The Spot, Good Food, Open 24 hours.* Turning back toward the car, Johnny called out to Claire, "Well? Are you coming or not?"

"Yes," she answered, closing the car door and crossing over to him on the sidewalk. He could see that Claire was still shaken.

"Look, the gas pedal got stuck. It wasn't my fault. I'll fix it when we get home." He smiled and held open the cafe door for her.

"Well, it was really scary going that fast," she said. Her lip trembled as if she was about to cry.

"Yeah, I know." And he *did* know. He didn't like being out of control any more than she did. The truth was that he'd had no control at all over the gas pedal.

Three truckers hunched over coffee and pie at the counter. A middle-aged waitress with red hair stood nearby, listening to the truckers talking. "Let's sit in a booth," suggested Johnny, leading Claire to one of the wooden stalls next to the window. He slid in and reached for a menu.

"I know what I want," announced Claire, her good mood returning. "Burger, fries, and a coke."

Before Johnny could decide, the waitress appeared. "What will you have?" she asked, taking a pencil from behind her ear and getting ready to write down their orders.

Claire recited her order. Johnny thought for a minute and then said he'd have the same. After the waitress had left, he added, "I miss Juan's Taco Stand down in L.A."

Claire nodded. "Mom says we just have to get used to things being different in a small town."

"Things *are* different here, that's for sure," snorted Johnny, glancing out the window at the GTO. Its chrome bumpers were shining like mirrors in the late afternoon sun.

In no time at all the waitress was back with their food. After putting the plates on the table, she stepped back and rested her hands on her hips. "Anything else I can get you?"

Johnny lifted the top off his burger and looked at the plain patty with lettuce and tomato. Not seeing what he wanted, he asked, "Could I get some thousand island dressing?"

"No problem." The waitress turned

and crossed the old linoleum floor and went through the swinging doors into the kitchen. On her way back to their table, she pressed a button on the jukebox that stood near the end of the counter. Patsy Cline, singing "I Fall To Pieces," blared out of the speaker.

"You kids like country western music?" asked the waitress. She reached over and gave Johnny a dish of thousand island dressing. "It's real popular in these parts."

"It's all right," said Johnny politely, giving his sister a look meant to keep her quiet.

But Claire wasn't good at keeping her mouth shut. She smiled sweetly. "If it's so popular, why don't they play it on the radio?"

"They do, sugar. K-Kountry 103 FM *only* plays country western," said the waitress, giving them a big smile.

Johnny kicked his sister under the table. She gave him a hard look, then explained. "Oh, well, we must have got the wrong station. My brother's radio only gets sixties music."

The waitress gave Johnny a funny look—as if she thought they were trying to pull her leg. "Really? That's *my* generation's music. I wouldn't mind hearing some of those oldies. I graduated from high school in 1965. What station were you tuned to?"

Before Claire could answer, one of the truckers called out for more coffee, forcing the waitress to hurry off.

"What did you have to say that for?" asked Johnny, biting into his burger.

"It's the truth," said Claire, her mouth stuffed with fries.

"I told you that the stations were probably all just playing sixties songs at the same time. Coincidence—you ever hear of that?" Johnny popped a french fry into his mouth and glared at his sister as if she were a moron.

Claire shrugged as they ate their food in silence and listened to Patsy Cline sing about lost love.

Drinking the last of his soda, Johnny leaned back on the wooden bench. His napkin slipped from his lap, and he reached down to retrieve it. Then he saw something that made his pulse race. Carved into the wooden bench was a heart, and inside the heart were the names *Johnny B.* and *Alice Lee.*

"Come on. Let's get out of here," said Johnny. All of a sudden, he felt uncomfortable. He had Johnny B.'s car and now he was sitting where Johnny B. had once sat. He crossed to the cash register and took out his wallet.

"That was fast," said the waitress, taking his money and ringing up the bill. "Used to be a time when kids liked to hang out here. I used to hang out here myself. Sipping cherry cokes, talking to my girlfriends, and flirting with the boys. This place used to really swing."

Johnny nodded politely as he backed toward the door. The air in the cafe seemed suddenly cold, bone-chilling cold. He shivered and glanced at the booth where he and Claire had just been sitting.

There he saw a young man wearing blue jeans and a white T-shirt, his black hair styled in a sixties flattop. The teenager was staring at Johnny with a strange, rather amused expression on his handsome face.

Johnny blinked hard. When he looked again, the booth was empty. *This is crazy*, he told himself. *Now I'm seeing things.*

Chapter 6

The first thing Johnny did when they got home was look under the car. But he couldn't see anything wrong. Claire watched him closely.

"I guess I'll have to take the car to a garage. They can put it up on a hoist, and I can see what's going on," he said as he straightened up.

"What about this door?" she asked. She pulled on the door handle and then on the window frame to see if the door would open. It stayed closed.

Johnny tried the door several times. It seemed perfectly fine. He shook his head. "Nothing wrong with it. Maybe it wasn't shut all the way or you hit the handle when we went into that turn."

Claire glared. "I closed it when we left the pool. I wasn't leaning on it. And I *didn't* touch the handle. I'm telling you it just flew open. Okay?"

Johnny nodded. He couldn't make sense of what had happened, but he didn't want to argue with Claire. And besides, he was sure there must be a logical explanation.

Claire started for the house, but then she turned and walked back. "I think your car is haunted or possessed or something. You know—like in those scary movies where the ghost won't leave the house."

"Oh, yeah, *right*, Claire. And next week, space aliens are going to land in that pasture out there," snorted Johnny, rolling his eyes.

"Well," shrugged Claire, "it *could* happen." She shot him a superior kind of look. Then, with a toss of her head, she turned and left him standing there.

He walked around the shiny black GTO, studying it from every angle. It looked like a sleek, black racing machine. *I don't know what happened out there, but this is one hot car*, he told himself. Then he took a dry rag from the pile he'd left on the lawn when he'd washed the car earlier. Slowly, he wiped the day's dust from the car's body.

"Dinner!" called his mother from the back porch.

"Coming!" Johnny gave the trunk of the car one last swipe with his rag. Then he crossed the lawn and went into the kitchen.

Johnny's father and sister were already at the dining room table when he sat down. He reached for the bowl of mashed potatoes.

"You should put on a shirt before you come to the table," said his father with a disapproving look.

"I know, Dad, but it's so hot. I feel

like I'm melting," argued Johnny.

His father used a napkin to wipe beads of sweat from his forehead. "Well, I'll excuse you just this once. But don't make it a habit." He picked up the platter of fried chicken and forked a piece onto his plate.

"Yes, sir," answered Johnny. He could see Claire smirking across the table, and he shot her a glare. As he dug into his dinner, he hoped that Claire wouldn't say anything about what had happened with the car. But it was too much to hope for. The minute their parents finished discussing their day, Claire started in.

Johnny groaned to himself and kept his eyes on his plate as Claire went on and on. She told them how the car's radio had played only sixties tunes. "It was *really* strange," she said, watching their faces for a reaction.

"Music from *our* generation?" their mother said with a smile.

Dr. Brown winked at his wife. "The deejays have a name for that." He seemed to think for a moment, and then he grinned and snapped his fingers. "I know—*a blast from the past*."

"But *every* station was playing a blast from the past," said Claire, a bit defensively.

"I told you it was a coincidence," Johnny said, trying to laugh it off. He wished she would just shut up, but she didn't. She went on to tell them how the gas pedal had stuck. Then she told how her door had flown open as they passed the cemetery.

Johnny's father put down his fork. He gave Johnny a sharp look. "When you got your license, you promised me you wouldn't speed."

"I wasn't speeding. The gas pedal got stuck. I'm going to take the car over to the gas station tomorrow and have them look at it."

"And the passenger door?" asked

his father, still looking concerned.

"I can't find anything wrong with it." Johnny shrugged.

"If you ask me, that car is haunted," Claire said.

Johnny glanced at his parents and made a circling sign by his head, as if telling them that Claire was crazy. "That's nonsense, Claire, and you know it," he said sternly.

"Oh yeah? What do we know about Johnny B.?" she asked.

Johnny quickly explained that they had found the name *Johnny B.* stenciled on the side of the car. He saw his parents exchange a silent, knowing look. "Do you know anything about him?" asked Johnny, wondering what the big secret was.

His father cleared his throat and frowned. "A little. Johnny B. was the Baers' only son. He died in an accident in 1965. The boy was just about your age then."

"What happened?" Claire and Johnny gasped at the same time.

Their father looked at their mother as if asking permission to go on. When she nodded, he continued, "Well, according to the realtor who sold us this house, Johnny B. sneaked out one night. He went over to the Lees' berry farm to pick up their daughter, Alice. It seems the two of them were going to elope. As they drove off, Farmer Lee ran after them with his shotgun. He was trying to scare them into stopping. Unfortunately, he tripped, and the gun went off. It shattered the back window of the car and killed the two teenagers instantly."

"Oh, that's *terrible!*" cried Claire.

So that's *where those little pock-marks around the back window frame came from,* thought Johnny.

"Just like I thought—the car is haunted," whispered Claire, looking more awed than frightened.

"I don't know about that, honey," chuckled their father. "I'm sure there's a logical explanation for everything that happened today."

"Maybe you should just get rid of that car, Johnny. After all, it was in an accident. They say that it crashed into a poplar tree," said his mother. She glanced from him to his father, hoping they would agree with her.

"No! I *love* that car," Johnny cried, pushing his chair back and standing up.

His father frowned. "Your mother is right, son. Sometimes, when a car has been in an accident, it never does run right again. How about I buy you that Honda you wanted?"

"No." He couldn't believe it. He had spent hours working on the GTO. It was a classic, a muscle car, and he loved it. "I don't want another car," snapped Johnny angrily.

"Watch your tone of voice, young man," warned his father, suddenly looking angry. His mother's face looked worried. Her eyes pleaded with Johnny to be reasonable.

Johnny didn't know what to say, so he turned and stormed out of the room.

Chapter 7

Johnny jumped into the GTO and turned the key in the ignition. Like always, the big engine roared to life. "There's nothing wrong with you," he told the car. He shifted into first gear and pressed down hard on the gas. Obediently, the GTO leapt forward. Down the drive it flew, spraying bits of gravel as it went.

Turning onto the empty, one-lane road, Johnny drove in the direction of Meridian Road. He couldn't believe that his parents wanted him to get rid of the car. Well, too bad. There was no way he was going to give it up.

The air streaming in the open window had cooled with the coming of evening. Johnny saw that the light was almost gone from the sky. He switched on the headlights, and the powerful beams lit up the road ahead. Shifting into fourth gear, he grinned as the car surged ahead in a burst of power.

Johnny flipped on the radio. The crackling, broken sound of static screeched from the speakers. Johnny shook his head and smiled. The car wasn't haunted. It just needed a new radio. Sure, they had gotten some stations earlier in the day, but that had just been a fluke.

Nearing the giant X-carved oak tree on Meridian Road, he thought back to that afternoon—how the GTO had sped up all on its own and rocketed down the road. The memory gave Johnny a tingling feeling of excitement in the pit of his stomach. He wanted to feel that speed again.

At the oak tree, he braked and let the car idle. He pictured Johnny B.

sitting behind the wheel, his right hand on the gearshift, his foot ready to hit the gas. Then suddenly Johnny jammed down hard on the gas pedal. The tires smoked as they grabbed for traction, and the GTO hurtled down the road. Johnny shifted through the gears, feeling the car speed up. Soon the speedometer was pushing a hundred.

"Yeah!" yelled Johnny, thrilled by the speed that made him feel so alive. *I'll bet Johnny B. won every race*, he thought, feeling a sudden kinship with the dead teenager.

Seeing the lights of an oncoming car in the distance, Johnny downshifted and slowed to the speed limit. *I'm keeping this car*, he vowed to himself.

He drove through the night without a destination, simply enjoying the solitude of the open road. Occasionally he passed a single light pole standing like a sentry at the end of a drive. He could see up the dirt roads to lonely farmhouses, their lighted windows the only sign of life.

Then the car's headlights glanced off an old metal mailbox, but not before Johnny saw the name—LEE'S BERRY FARM. Slamming on the brakes, he made a U-turn and drove back. For a moment he sat staring at the name on the mail box. *This has to be the old Lee place—where Alice Lee lived*, he thought. Sitting back from the road beyond a stand of poplar trees, the big old house was dark. He turned the car into the lane.

The GTO bounced down the dirt road. Tall weeds rose up like ghosts in the car's headlights and made a swooshing sound as the car flattened them. *No one has been down this road for a long time*, thought Johnny. Suddenly, he felt a bit uneasy. Past the grove of poplar trees and beyond what had once been a lawn was an old house. Switching off the engine, he got out and walked toward the old house. It looked like it was rotting away, one board at a time. The windows were broken, and the front door had come off its hinges and fallen to the porch. Johnny stared into the dark interior. He saw nothing but darkness. Suddenly a deep sadness filled his chest. He knew it was for Alice Lee and Johnny B., two teenagers he'd never met.

As Johnny was thinking about the teenagers who'd tried to elope, the GTO's engine roared to life. Surprised, Johnny turned and watched in utter amazement as the car started down the dirt road for the highway. As he took off after it, the car's back window suddenly shattered into a million tiny pieces. Glass flew everywhere. Then, still on its own, the car veered left and crashed into a poplar tree!

Johnny ran to the idling car and saw that it was empty. Of course. But the light from the radio panel glowed eerily as Chuck Berry twanged his guitar and sang, "Go, Johnny go. Go, go, Johnny B. Goode."

The interior of the car was cold. *Cold as death*, Johnny thought. Horror spread through the boy's mind as he stepped away from the GTO. Fear gripped his chest as he stood shivering in the hot night.

Then Johnny started running like he'd never run before in his life. When he reached the highway, he looked back. The headlights on the GTO had gone out. The Lee place was dark again, dark as the inside of a grave.